Gila monsters meet you at the airport

By Marjorie Weinman Sharmat   Pictures by Byron Barton

ALADDIN PAPERBACKS

Aladdin Paperbacks
An imprint of Simon & Schuster
Children's Publishing Division
1230 Avenue of the Americas
New York, NY 10020
First Aladdin Paperbacks edition, 1990
A hardcover edition of *Gila Monsters Meet You at the Airport* is
available from Simon & Schuster Children's Publishing Division.
Printed in Hong Kong

15   14

Library of Congress Cataloging-in-Publication Data

Sharmat, Marjorie Weinman.
Gila monsters meet you at the airport / by Marjorie Weinman Sharmat;
pictures by Byron Barton.—1st Aladdin ed.
p.   cm.
Summary: A New York City boy's preconceived ideas of life in the
West make him very apprehensive about the family's move there.
ISBN 0-689-71383-5
[1. West (U.S.)—Fiction.] I. Barton, Byron, ill. II. Title.
[PZ7.S5299Gi 1990]
[E]—dc20   89-38398

For Roz,
who grew up to be an artist

« 1 »

I live at 165 East 95th Street, New York City,
and I'm going to stay here forever.

My mother and father are moving. Out West.

They say I have to go, too.
They say I can't stay here forever.

Out West nobody plays baseball because they're
too busy chasing buffaloes.

And there's cactus everywhere you look.
But if you don't look, you have to stand up
just as soon as you sit down.

Out West it takes fifteen minutes just to say hello.
Like this: H-O-W-W-W-D-Y, P-A-A-A-R-D-N-E-R.

Out West I'll look silly all the time.
I'll have to wear chaps and spurs and a bandanna
and a hat so big that nobody can find me underneath it.
And I'll have to ride a horse to school every day
and I don't know how.

Out West everybody grows up to be a sheriff.
I want to be a subway driver.

My best friend is Seymour, and we like to eat
salami sandwiches together.
Out West I probably won't have any friends,
but if I do, they'll be named Tex or Slim,
and we'll eat chili and beans for breakfast. And lunch.
And dinner. While I miss Seymour and salami.

« 2 »

I'm on my way. Out West.
It's cool in the airplane.

The desert is so hot you can collapse, and then
the buzzards circle overhead, but no one rescues
you because it's real life and not the movies.
There are clouds out the window.
No buzzards yet.

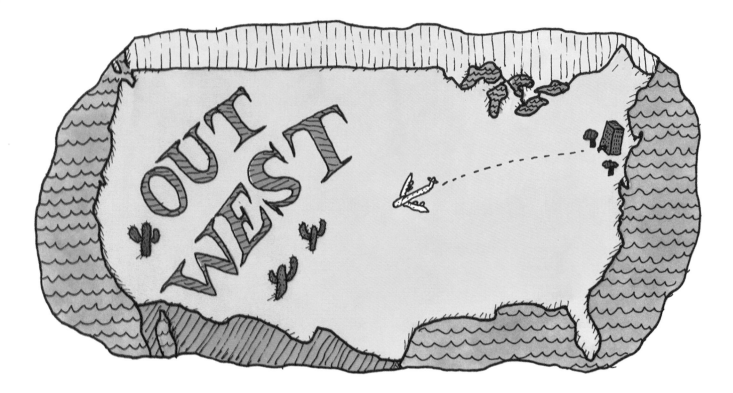

I'm looking at a map.
Before, whenever I looked at a map, I always knew
my house was on the right.
But no more.
Now I'm in the middle of that map,
and I'm going left, left. Out West.

Seymour says there are Gila monsters and horned toads out West,
and I read it in a book so I know it's so.
But Seymour says they meet you at the airport.

« 3 »

We're here.
Out West.
I don't know what a Gila monster or horned toad looks like,
but I don't think I see any at the airport.

I see a boy in a cowboy hat.

He looks like Seymour, but I know his name is Tex.

"Hi," I say.

"Hi," he says. "I'm moving East."

"Great!" I say.

"Great?" he says. "What's so great about it? Don't you know that the streets are full of gangsters? They all wear flowers in their lapels so they look honest, but they zoom around in big cars with screeching brakes. You have to jump out of their way.

"In the East it snows and blows all the time,
except for five minutes when it's spring and summer.

"And you have to live on the 50th floor. Airplanes fly
through your bedroom, and you've got to duck fast.

"They ran out of *extra* space in the East a long time ago.
It's so crowded people sit on top of each other when they
ride to work.

"And alligators live in the sewers. I read it in a book
so I know it's so."

Then the mother and father of the boy who looks like Seymour
but isn't grab his hand, and he goes off.
"Sometimes the alligators get out," he yells to me. "And
they wait for you at the airport."

« 4 »

It's warm, but there's a nice breeze.
We're in a taxi riding to our new house.

No horses yet.
I don't see any buffalo stampedes either.

I see a restaurant just like the one in my old
neighborhood.

I *see* some kids playing baseball.

I see a horse. Hey, that's a great-looking horse!
I'm going to ask my mother and father for one like it.